Margaret Clark

Illustrated by Bettina Guthridge

 sundance

Published by
Sundance Publishing
234 Taylor Street
Littleton, MA 01460

Project commissioned and managed by
Lorraine Bambrough-Kelly, The Writer's Style
Designed by Cath Lindsey/design rescue

First published 1997 by
Addison Wesley Longman Australia Pty Limited
95 Coventry Street
South Melbourne 3205 Australia
Exclusive United States Distribution: Sundance Publishing

ISBN 0-7608-1934-3

PRINTED IN CANADA

CONTENTS

CHAPTER 1
Last . . . and Liking It

Luke was always last. It didn't matter what was happening—something always made him late or last.

"Hurry up, Luke. Your toast is getting cold!" Mom called.

Luke always tried to be last to breakfast. He didn't like his toast too hot because the butter would melt and make his toast soggy.

And he didn't like to watch his sister, Jane, heaping horrible apricot jam on her toast, or slurping her milk through her missing front teeth. It was so gross!

And he hated the way his baby brother, Thomas, would spit cereal, dribble orange juice, and finger paint with the peanut butter that had started out on his toast!

“Hurry up, Luke, and get in the car.
It’s time for school!”
yelled Dad.

Luke grabbed his schoolbag and wandered out to the car. Jane made a face at him because she was first, and so she got to sit in the front.

But Luke *liked* sitting in the back. He could see everything that was happening out of all the windows.

"Hurry up and get in line, Luke," called his teacher, as the bell rang to go into school. "One day you just might surprise me and be first!"

But Luke *liked* to be the last in line. He could pick up things that the other kids had dropped and give them back to them.

"It's an exciting day," said Luke's teacher, Mrs. Michaels. "Did you all remember? We're going to the zoo. Hurry up and get on the bus."

Luke was last in line, as usual. And when he finally climbed up the steps and onto the bus, there were no seats left because some of the mothers had come on the field trip, too.

"Just sit up front next to the driver," said Mrs. Michaels. She was way in the back with Emma Evangaline, cleaning up—because Emma had already thrown up.

Luke got off the bus first. It was strange being first. He didn't like it much.

Amanda Brown stepped on his heel, and his shoe came off. Mrs. Michaels pressed her lips together, which meant she was about to lose her cool. "Hurry up and put on your shoe," she said angrily.

Luke had to stay behind, put his shoe on again, and do up the laces.

CHAPTER 2
At the Zoo

Last in the line again, Luke felt happy. They went to see the elephants, and the biggest one was in a bad mood. It squirted black gooey stuff all over Sarah Diaz's best blue dress, and she screamed her head off.

EAGLES
ELEPHANTS

“Be quiet, Sarah. It’ll wash off,” snapped Mrs. Michaels. She hurried them all away from the elephants.

Luke was last, of course. He picked up the doughnut Sarah had dropped and threw it to the baby elephant. The big elephant trumpeted so loudly that Luke nearly jumped through the sky. But it was great fun.

At the ostriches, Ben Borgani teased the biggest ostrich by strutting and jerking his elbows up and down. It fluffed up its feathers angrily and charged at the fence. Everyone screamed. Mrs. Michaels went ballistic at Ben, and then she hurried them all away.

Luke was last in the line again. He was able to pick up the beautiful feather that the ostrich had dropped. He put it in his bag.

They all arrived at the gorilla's cage. Ben Borgani made faces and jumped up and down in front of the gorilla. "Hey, King Kong, can you play Ping-Pong?" he yelled. Then he took off his cap and threw it into the cage. Everyone laughed.

Mrs. Michaels went ape! She made them all move on. Luke was at the end of the line, so he was able to pick up Ben's cap when the gorilla threw it back.

"Mrs. Michaels, Mrs. Michaels," he called. But she wasn't listening, so Luke put the cap in his bag.

"Hurry up, Luke," called Mrs. Michaels, as they walked toward the picnic area. "We're going to have our lunch."

CHAPTER 3
Catch Up, Luke!

Luke sat by a tree, eating slowly. Everyone else finished and Mrs. Michaels took them off to play baseball. Luke finally finished and started after them.

But, on the way, he saw some people who were busy with cameras and overhead microphones. They were making a TV program about the zoo.

"Could you just walk over there and hold out this bread to those geese?" said a man wearing a floppy hat, to Luke.

So Luke did as he was asked.

Mrs. Michaels came rushing back. She thought that Luke was getting attacked by the geese.

But the man asked her to sign a piece of paper so that Luke could appear on TV.

"Stay with the group, please, Luke," said Mrs. Michaels.

She went rushing off to stop Ben Borgani from putting his fingers in the aviary.

The other kids were near the kangaroos. Luke wandered across to look, too, just as the rest of the class walked off with Mrs. Michaels.

A baby kangaroo had climbed out of its mother's pouch and gotten its head stuck in the fence. Luke told a zookeeper. The zookeeper rescued the baby kangaroo and gave Luke some special zoo postcards. Luke proudly put them in his bag.

Everyone else was at the wombat enclosure. Ben Borgani put his foot under the fence, and a hungry wombat tried to bite his shoe.

Mrs. Michaels was very busy making everyone line up.

"From now on, you can walk in front with me, Ben Borgani," she said angrily. "And so can you, Luke. Then you won't be last."

Luke walked down the path at the front of the line with Mrs. Michaels and Ben Borgani. They came to the snake house. Amanda Brown started screaming. She was NOT going into the snake house. Mrs. Michaels went to comfort Amanda.

Ben Borgani went in the exit and everyone followed him.

"We're going the wrong way!" yelled Luke.

So they turned around and went back.
Now Luke was last again.

Luke bent down to pull up his socks. As he straightened up, he saw a snake shedding its skin through the window of the Deadly Snakes cage.

“Would you like the skin?” asked a zoo-keeper who was walking past.

Luke nodded. The keeper picked up the skin and gave it to him. Luke put it in his bag.

He caught up to the others and watched the otters dive for fish. Ben Borgani tried to climb up the side of the tank for a closer look. He fell in, head first. Mrs. Michaels hauled him out.

They went to see the giraffe eat leaves from a tall tree. Emma Evangaline bent her neck far back to look and started crying. She said she couldn't bend it forward. Mrs. Michaels rubbed it to make it feel better.

They moved on to see the sleeping bears and the jumping frogs. They saw all the animals at the zoo — except the performing seals.

"Everyone must use the rest rooms before getting on the bus," ordered Mrs. Michaels.

When Luke came out, everyone had gone. He walked to the exit and saw the bus driving away. Mrs. Michaels must have forgotten to count them.

CHAPTER 4
Left Behind

Luke sighed. What should he do? Then he looked at his watch. It was performance time for the seals, so he walked down the path to the seal tank.

The seals were awesome. One seal threw a little hoop in the air and Luke caught it. The seal clapped for Luke with its flippers, and the crowd clapped for Luke and the seal. The seal trainer gave Luke the hoop to keep. He put it in his bag.

The seal trainer noticed that Luke was by himself. “Where’s your teacher?” he asked.

Luke explained that the bus had gone without him.

“I’ll phone your school,” said the seal trainer. “Then while you’re waiting to be picked up, you can help me feed the seals. And after that we can have an afternoon snack.”

The taxi finally arrived to take Luke back to school.

When they arrived back at the school, Mrs. Michaels was looking very worried and tired. She gave Luke a big hug.

"I wonder if going to the zoo is worth all the trouble," Mrs. Michaels said to the class. "What did you notice? What did you find?"

Luke went up to the front with his bag. He took out the things he had collected at the zoo. He showed everyone the ostrich feather, the zoo cards, the snake skin, *and* the seal's hoop that he had been given. And he gave Ben Borgani back his hat. Luke's friends were very impressed.

Mrs. Michaels sighed. "Sometimes you are just plain lucky, Luke."

Luke smiled. *He* knew why he liked to be last.

Lucky last Luke Last. He had to live up to his name!

ABOUT THE AUTHOR

Margaret Clark

Margaret Clark is a well-known author of books for children and teenagers. Her first book, *Pugwall,* was published in 1987 and was subsequently made into a television series. Since then, she has had fifty books published and is now a full-time author.

Margaret lives with her husband and a dog called Girlie and a black and white cat called Domino. She is currently working toward a doctorate in education.

Margaret's goal is to be happy in whatever she does.

ABOUT THE ILLUSTRATOR

Bettina Guthridge

Bettina Guthridge grew up in Australia. After studying art and teaching for three years, she moved to Italy with her husband. Ten years and two children later, Bettina and her family returned to Australia where she began illustrating children's books.

Bettina has illustrated many books for children—books written by well-known children's authors such as Ogden Nash and Roald Dahl. Her first book, *Matilda and the Dragon*, was followed by *Hurry Up Oscar.*

Bettina has had two successful exhibitions of sculptures made from objects she found on the beach. Her special pet is a border collie named Tex.